# ONE FELL SOUP

STREET FOOD COZIES, BOOK 9

GRETCHEN ALLEN

SUMMER PRESCOTT BOOKS PUBLISHING

**Copyright 2023 Summer Prescott Books**

All Rights Reserved. No part of this publication nor any of the information herein may be quoted from, nor reproduced, in any form, including but not limited to: printing, scanning, photocopying, or any other printed, digital, or audio formats, without prior express written consent of the copyright holder.

\*\*This book is a work of fiction. Any similarities to persons, living or dead, places of business, or situations past or present, is completely unintentional.

## CHAPTER 1

"I'm sorry but I don't think I really get it," Rhonda Knapp whispered to Billie Halifax. They walked along the beach toward the boardwalk and the newly installed Wilted Lettuce Vegan food truck manned by the latest member of the food truck family, Toren Smart.

"What part don't you get, exactly?" Billie asked. She was grateful for the company and patient enough with her friend that the question didn't bother her. Coming from anyone else, Billie might not have been able to say the same.

"Okay," Rhonda said, stopping where she walked. "Why not just have a salad truck? I adore that salad place on the mainland. I forget the name, but you know where I mean. You go there and you build your salad with whatever you can think of. They have everything!"

Billie smiled. "I know the place," she said.

"See? Why not just have a mini version of that restaurant in a food truck?" Rhonda asked. "Heck, I'd probably eat there at least once a day. Why do you need veggie burgers and veggie tacos and veggie chicken sandwiches? It seems so redundant."

"For one thing, these are not the 'veggie burgers' of twenty years ago," Billie explained. "We call this 'plant-based' meat or chicken or whatever. Have you seen the number of fast food chains hopping on board? These meat-substitute foods are a whole lot different than you might think."

"Yeah, okay," she said and resumed her walk. "I get that it's different from the stuff I've tried in the past, but I still don't get why you couldn't just open a salad truck."

"Toren is going to serve salads," Billie said. "You were there the other night when he shared his menu."

"I know," Rhonda said. "I guess I just don't get the rest of it. You have a taco truck. Why do you need vegan tacos on a vegan truck?"

"What if you're with your family on the island for a vacation or a festival, like the Holistic Fair this weekend, and everyone else wants to walk down to the boardwalk for tacos for lunch, but you can't because you happen to be vegan?"

"Well, then, I guess you can have a salad," Rhonda said.

Billie dropped her head and sighed. "You are impossible," she said. "No, you go to the vegan truck for a taco. Or a burger. Or a chicken sandwich and soup. Whatever your little plant-based heart desires."

"Alright, I suppose that does make sense," Rhonda said. "I just expected him to serve more gourmet dishes than a simple taco or a burger or a chicken sandwich."

Billie chuckled. She spotted the food trucks, all nine of them, lined up along the boardwalk. Not all of them were operational at the moment. It was just past eight in the morning, and she was out for her morning walk with Waffles, the Tibetan Mastiff she had inherited after the death of his owner. For once, Waffles behaved himself on the other end of the leash. It was Rhonda who was giving her fits that morning.

"Part of the appeal of having the vegan truck on the island is to provide a plant-based alternative for everyday foods," Billie said, and not for the first time in their conversation. "Toren will have a variety of gourmet daily specials, not to mention the crepes and the charcuterie boards."

"Okay, one, how do you have vegan crepes? Aren't those egg-based?" Rhonda asked, stopping again, this time with her hand on her hip. "And two, can you please for once explain to me just what the heck a charcuterie board is? All I see is a bunch of cut up food on a board!"

Billie threw her head back and laughed. "That's basically what a charcuterie board is. It's a snack tray, or an appetizer tray usually meant to be enjoyed during a wine tasting or on a picnic," Billie said. "It's not like just going into your fridge at home and cutting up a bunch of veggies on a tray, though. You have dips and sauces and breads and olives and pickles, too. Traditional boards even have a variety of smoked meats sometimes."

"Just not these," Rhonda said, pointing to the vegan truck.

"Now you're catching on," Billie said. She picked up the pace and walked past her friend.

"Did I make you mad?" Rhonda asked, catching up with her. "I don't want you to be mad at me."

"You didn't make me mad, you made me hungry after talking about all that food." Billie smiled. "Let's eat."

"It's too early," Rhonda said. "Hardly any of the trucks are open."

"That's true, but it's also why I want to take Waffles back home and then go into the commissary kitchen to make breakfast," Billie said. "Don't forget that I'm a trained chef as well."

Rhonda nodded eagerly. "You hardly ever cook for us! What are we having? I think I'm in the mood for a Denver omelet myself."

Billie smiled and directed the dog across the sand toward the gate into the festival grounds. She had to walk him carefully to avoid the many people already milling about the grounds to prepare for the Holistic Fair set to begin in two days.

So many vendors decided to rent space that Asher Scanlan, her business partner and boyfriend, had pushed the idea of directing participants to the boardwalk for meals rather than move the food trucks onto the festival grounds for convenience. "We need to save as much space as we can," Asher had told her. She agreed and so did most of her managers. A few had even suggested coupons to encourage business, since folks would have to go a bit further for food.

"Let's go and see what we can rustle up, then," Billie said as they headed straight for her tiny house. Waffles resisted a little when she stopped to open the gate to the dog pen. Recently she had added a pad of sod just to give him the extra luxury of grass along with the sand he was used to. Waffles retreated to his mini mansion of a dog house with a pout, but it didn't take him long to settle in.

"You give that dog too much," Rhonda said.

"Oh, come on," Billie said as they walked toward the large, metal building in the middle of the festival grounds. The center of the building was divided into ten separate test kitchens. A large pantry, several smaller storage rooms, walk-in coolers, and freezers also surrounded the kitchen's expanse. Billie's office was on one end of the building and Asher's was on the other.

When they walked inside Billie could hear the din of noises. She had a feeling most of the test kitchens were occupied at the moment. Several of her food truck managers used them for their morning prep work before opening their food trucks just before lunch.

"Something smells good in here," Billie said when she entered the kitchen space. She smiled at Marcel Johnson, her taco truck manager. He stood, cutting up several bunches of cilantro to add to his island-famous Pico de Gallo.

"What are you here for this morning?" Marcel asked her.

"Breakfast." Billie grinned. "Namely, Denver

omelets." She nodded at Rhonda who had pulled up a chair close to the counter.

"Oh, are you accepting orders?" Marcel asked.

"Orders for what?" Dillon Frazier called out from the farthest kitchen space. He stood chopping smoked brisket alongside his sous chef, Olivia Mason.

"Omelets!" Billie waved her arms to invite him and the others over. "I'll whip up a few. Everyone okay with peppers, onions, and sharp cheddar cheese?"

"Sounds good to me," Cameron Shields said. He looked up from his burger press, the latest contraption he had purchased to speed up the morning prep work for the burger truck he managed.

"I'll take a big one," Toren Smart called from his kitchen station. The decision had been made to postpone the official grand opening of the truck until the following weekend, but he had wanted to make sure the truck was open for the onslaught of holistic living enthusiasts.

"You? Um, I hate to be the one to have to tell you this, but eggs aren't exactly vegan," Liza Sheridan called out. Her own counter space was filled with chopped fruit for the ice cream truck she operated with her twin sister, Polly.

Toren stood up to his full height. He was two

inches shorter than Billie and reminded her of a Victorian-era school teacher. "Yes, I am aware of that." He chuckled. "I may run a vegan food truck, and I absolutely take a lot of pride in the plant-based items I create fresh every day, but I am a vegetarian, not a strict vegan. I would adore a vegetable omelet if you don't mind."

Billie smiled and nodded. "Coming right up," she said and began cracking eggs into a large metal mixing bowl.

"So, your veggie burgers and chicken patties aren't frozen from a box?" Rhonda asked from her seat.

Toren knit his eyebrows at her and frowned. "Allow me to say, this is not a 'veggie burger,' as you call it," he said. "I make them fresh daily just as your burger food truck manager might do. My recipe includes shiitake mushrooms, shallots, walnuts, brown rice, and a whole lot of savory spices. When you get the chance to try one, let me know if it tastes like any veggie burger you've ever had before. I think you'll be pleasantly surprised."

"Deal," Rhonda promised. "I'm always open to trying new things."

"Here you go," Marcel said. He set a large bowl

of diced onions and peppers in front of Billie. "I had a few leftovers, and I thought they might help."

"Thank you, Marcel."

"Could you use some chopped garlic and shallots?" Dillon picked up a cutting board halfway filled with ingredients.

"Bring it on over," Billie said.

"And we have some extra black peppercorns and sweet corn," Polly offered. "I overestimated the ingredients for the sweet corn and black pepper variety we're debuting this week."

"You two and your ice cream recipes." Rhonda shook her head. "You are the most creative girls I have ever met. Pepper and sweet corn in ice cream. I mean, who knew?"

"Thank you," Polly and Liza said in unison.

Billie stirred in the shallots and threw her head back. "This reminds me of a story my grandmother used to tell me," she said. "All about a village that came together to make a huge pot of soup when a stranger came to town with nothing, and in the end, they had enough for everyone."

"Stone Soup! I remember that story," Olivia said. "My grandmother told me all about it, too."

Billie dished out the omelets as soon as they were

ready. Rhonda was served first, and herself last. She moved her plate to a large, round table in the middle of the eating area. She was quickly joined by several other members of her staff. The only thing missing was Asher.

"Billie? Are you in here?" Detective Sullivan asked from the hallway. Her red hair was loose around her shoulders, not a look Billie had seen before. "We have a little problem outside."

"What's going on?" Billie asked. The first bite of her omelet was still on the end of her fork.

"Two of your vendors are in a pretty heated argument about who is in the right space," she said. "I figured I ought to come and get you to settle things."

Billie groaned and set her fork down on her plate. She stood and quickly ran for the diagram in Asher's office. "Lead the way," she said to the detective and followed her out the door.

## CHAPTER 2

"I booked this space," a tall and lanky dark-haired woman with close-cropped hair said. She placed herself between the detective and Billie. Her arms were crossed over her chest. "I paid for this space, and I intend to use it."

"And your name is?" Billie asked. The woman simply stared at her.

"Ma'am," Detective Sullivan prompted. "What is your name?"

"Whitley Carson," she said.

"And what is your name?" Billie asked the other woman, who was standing with her arms folded as well. Unlike Whitley, she was a much shorter woman with a wide girth and a pleasant face. Her blonde hair was swept up on top of her head in a loose updo. She waved her arms around as she spoke. "As I told your detective here, my name is Kelly Peck and I am the one who paid for this site, and the one adjoining it. We have a hot yoga seminar every hour during these fairs, and I always book two spaces to accommodate the tents."

"No. I booked the space close to the restrooms because I serve herbal teas among other things and my clientele often need fast access to the facilities," Whitley said. Billie pushed the chart in front of Sully's gaze.

"Here is site six-oh-two," Billie pointed out. "I have one Whitley Carson marked down here. Kelly Peck is here and there." She pointed to the site next to the one in question, and the site across the road.

"Now, what sort of sense does that make?" Kelly asked. She threw her arms over her head and turned in a complete circle as she spoke. The long layers of her outfit fanned out as she turned. "Why on earth would I book two sites for myself that are separated by a road?"

"When you booked them, you should have received a confirmation email that included a full color map of the area," Billie said. She cursed Asher for taking off just before the fair and leaving her there to deal with the mess on her own. She opened her phone and pressed a few buttons until she found the email thread. "I just checked, and I see that you replied to the email and said that it all looked just fine to you."

"Well, I guess things are settled now," Sully said.

"Well, how was I supposed to know the sites were across the road from each other? I can't read a map," Kelly shouted. "It's not my fault this happened."

"I understand, but you did okay it via email," Billie reminded her. "I'm afraid I can't take responsibility for the fact that you couldn't read the map."

"This is not fair," Kelly said. "Why can't she just take the single site across the road and allow me the two sites next to each other? Clearly, you can see that I need two adjoining sites!" She turned to Billie.

"I'm afraid that I can't force her to do that," Billie said, not clearly seeing anything "If you are willing, Whitley, I would refund part of your deposit fee."

"I think I will stay right here, thank you," Whitley said and turned back to her site.

"I'm sorry, Ms. Peck," Billie said. "I'm afraid that my hands are tied."

"What about my refund? Don't I get that offer as well since I've been so greatly inconvenienced?" Kelly asked.

Sully cleared her throat. "That was by your own

choice, ma'am. I don't think you are owed anything in this matter."

"Fine," Kelly said. "I will inform my clientele that they have to get ready in this tent and then traipse across the road half naked so they can participate in hot yoga. That makes a lot of sense."

"You probably should have considered that before you set things up the way you did," Whitley suggested, without looking at them.

"Why can't you just have your clients change in the same tent they are going to do the yoga class in?" Sully asked.

"Because that isn't the way I want it set up." Kelly picked up her long, layered skirt and headed off back down the road toward the other side of the festival grounds.

Billie shrugged and held the diagram close to her chest. "I really wish Asher was here instead of with his family," she said.

"Is that because you miss him or because you'd rather him be here to deal with this headache?" Sully asked as they walked back toward the metal building.

"Of course, I miss him, but yeah, kinda. Dealing with this sort of thing isn't exactly at the top of my skillset," Billie admitted. "Now, if you don't mind, let's hurry it up a little. My eggs are probably already cold, and I don't like eating cold eggs."

"Jeez. Hangry much?" Sully joked as she picked up her pace.

Back inside the commissary kitchen, the rest of the truck managers had already eaten and cleared their plates. "I put your plate in the warmer," Dillon announced when she walked inside. "I hope you don't mind."

"Mind? She was ready to strangle someone if she couldn't get back here before they got too cold." Sully laughed. "I was a little afraid to come in here to find them already frozen."

"I'm not that bad," Billie said. She looked around the room for support, but only found several pairs of averted eyes. "What? I like warm food. Sue me!"

"What was going on outside?" Dillon asked. He brought Billie's plate over from the warmer.

"Two fair vendors were arguing over spaces," Billie said.

"Sounds pretty normal," Dillon said and chuckled. "Asher has said to me that you can't have a multiple day event without at least one person throwing a fit about where they are supposed to set up."

"Really? He never complains to me," Billie said,

wondering just how much drama Asher had saved her from. She still hadn't taken a bite of her eggs.

"He probably wouldn't," Dillon said. "You generally have your hands full as it is with all of us and our worries and concerns."

"Speak for yourself, Frazier," Marcel called from the other side of the room. "I'm her golden child."

"You only think you're the favorite, Johnson," Carl piped up to say. He had arrived just in time to roll out his first few batches of sushi for the truck he managed. The rest were made on demand, on site.

"Well, now that we've heard from the problem children, I think we should head out to the boardwalk," Isa Carello said to the Sheridan twins. "It's okay, guys. We all know who the favorite is!"

"I'm the favorite," Rhonda said. "And I know that's true because you all cook and bake for me without question. But sadly, I have to leave all this and open up my own store front. See you all later."

"Don't forget to stop by after," Toren called out. "I promise you will think very differently about vegan food if you do."

"Challenge accepted," Rhonda said as she made her way to the door. She turned to Billie before she left. "Don't you let any of this get you down. If you need help while Asher is out of town, you know where to find me."

"That goes double for me, Boss," Dillon said. "I have a sous chef who can keep things going if I need to step out."

"There you go," Sully said. She smiled and patted Billie on the shoulder. "By the way, how many more food trucks are you going to add? Aren't you afraid you'll run out of room down there on the boardwalk?"

Billie chuckled. She shoved a bite of omelet in her mouth and smiled. "We have three more to go, and no, I will never run out of room for the best street food in the world."

## CHAPTER 3

Billie woke up before sunrise early the next morning. She sat on the edge of her bed and sighed, stretching her arms high over her head. Despite the fact that Asher was out of town, and she was by herself for the first time running a fair, she had a good feeling about the day. She rushed to the shower and emerged a few minutes later. The day called for comfortable clothes and a simple hairstyle, she decided.

A few minutes later, Billie plucked the leash off of the hook by the fridge and called for Waffles. He was cuddled on a blanket in front of the couch.

"Come on, buddy," Billie repeated, this time in a high-pitched voice. Waffles covered his head with his paws and groaned. "Let's go for a walk." Waffles continued to ignore her until she scratched behind his ears for a solid minute. It was then that he perked up enough to go for a walk.

They headed along the fence toward the gate, careful to avoid the vendor areas on the festival grounds. Billie smiled when she saw the first pink hues of the sunrise in the sky. She steered Waffles toward the southern point on the beach where she often let him off the leash to run in the water. This morning, she decided it was a little too dark and a little too early to allow him to go too far, but she allowed him to play for a bit, knowing just how much he loved it.

When they headed back toward the festival grounds, Billie paused when she saw the outline of another large yacht at the marina. Several more would probably arrive over the next twenty-four hours, she figured. The Holistic Fair was a big draw for a number of people, including small cruise ships that filled the gulf with wealthy passengers. Billie was familiar enough with the sort of fair attendees that would inhabit the island over the coming long weekend.

"Let's go," she said to the dog when she had watched the boat long enough. Waffles was more awake and more interested in the crabs skittering along the beach. He resisted a little when she pulled the leash to direct him back home. It was a little later than she had wanted it to be when she secured the dog in his pen and headed toward the commissary kitchen. Like the previous morning, she'd expected to see several of her truck managers prepping for their trucks for the day. Although the fair wasn't slated to start until the following day, the island was teeming with vendors and fairgoers. Billie had already heard Isa, Dillon, and Cam mention opening their trucks a couple of hours earlier than normal. Enid and the Sheridan twins planned to stay open past their typical closing time as well.

"Good morning," Olivia Mason called to her when she walked into the kitchen space.

"Morning," Billie said. "Looks like the boss has you busy pretty early."

Olivia said nothing but rolled her eyes and offered a grin. Dillon rushed in behind her with a stack of ribs from the cooler. Billie returned Olivia's grin and headed back to her office. After the fiasco she fended off the day before, she wanted to remind herself of the vendors who had paid for more than one space. More than half of the vendors had already been on the island for a full day, but the remainder should come in over the coming hours.

Her plan was to walk around and check in with

the vendors who were already there. She'd casually double checked that the diagram she had of their spaces matched their expectations upon arrival. She also planned to check in with Whitley and Kelly just to make sure there were no lingering hard feelings. It was just before eight when she headed back out with the diagram in hand.

"Good morning," she called to Whitley when she spotted her coming down the walkway toward her tent. "How is everything going?"

"Oh, you know," Whitley said. She carried a case of bottled water in her thin arms. "Just getting things ready for tomorrow." She opened the flap to her tent and walked inside with the water. Billie peeked in behind her. She was always amazed at the worlds that could be created inside a canopy tent. Some vendors went so far as to recreate the interior of luxury spaces or palatial resorts inside of their tents.

Whitley's space was no exception. Billie could see a chaise lounge in one corner and a series of clear glass water coolers against the wall. The aroma of spice and herbs wafted out of the space.

"Can I help you with something?" Whitley asked.

"Oh, no," Billie said, blushing slightly. "I was just trying to place that scent. Vanilla? Maybe cloves and cinnamon?"

"All of the above, and then some," Whitley said. "Have a good day." She whipped the tent flap closed in Billie's face.

"Well, then," Billie muttered. She turned around and decided she may as well check with the other troubled vendor, Kelly, next. The vendor's business, "Yoga Hot and Cold," occupied tents on either side of the roadway. Billie was unsure which tent she should check first. She thought she could hear noise from the side closest to Whitley's tent.

"Hello? Ms. Peck." Billie approached the entrance to the tent and called out again. She hesitated, and then pushed the flap open with her hand.

"Can I help you?"

Billie jumped when she heard the voice behind her. She turned around and smiled at the unfamiliar woman. "I was just looking for Kelly Peck," she said.

"Okay, well, I'm her business partner, Tiffany," the woman said.

"Oh, nice to meet you." Billie held out her hand to the other woman, but the woman declined to shake it.

"And you are?"

"Sorry. Billie Halifax," she said. "Co-owner of the very ground you are standing on."

"Is there something you need?" Tiffany asked.

Billie noticed her looking past her at the other tent across the road.

"Like I said, I'm looking for Kelly. There was a little disagreement yesterday with another vendor and I wanted to check in with her to see if she found her accommodations satisfactory."

"Satisfactory, yes," Tiffany replied. "What she requested, no."

Billie was taken a little off guard by the woman. She glanced down at the diagram of the spaces in her hands and picked up the top pages to the email correspondence between Asher and Kelly Peck she had printed off, just in case she needed to refer to it.

"What was your name again?" Billie asked. She searched for a different name in the emails, but only found Kelly's.

"Tiffany Bonner. Kelly's business partner," she snapped.

"Sorry, I was just looking over the information I have here," Billie said. "You know, there was a conversation that took place between Kelly and my business partner, Asher. He's the one who plans and schedules vendor placement for the majority of our festivals. I've looked over their emails and I think there must have been a misunderstanding on Kelly's part. She had access to a three-dimensional layout of the festival grounds and illustrations that indicated where her spaces were located."

"What does all of that mean?" Tiffany asked. She was clearly preoccupied with something and didn't want to be bothered.

"It means that while I'm sorry about the inconvenience, in the future, I would encourage her to look more carefully before agreeing to things," Billie said. "I wish I could remedy the situation more to her liking, but that would mean changing the space another vendor approved and paid for as well. It's just not possible. I hope you both understand."

Tiffany sighed. For the first time, she focused her attention directly on their conversation. "Well, to say that my business partner is not attuned to detail would be a falsehood," she said. "I instruct many of our classes and deal with the wellness side of our business while she runs the books and marketing campaigns. Once in a while, Kelly drops the ball. Just like the rest of us do, I suppose, but she is a dear friend of mine and I adore her. She's fantastic at what she does."

Billie nodded. "Of course," she said. "That's one reason I wanted to look over things and make sure I knew what really happened. I went through the emails for that reason alone. We are all capable of misunderstanding, I suppose."

Whitley stepped out of her tent. "Where is your partner?" she asked Tiffany. There was no acknowledgment of Billie standing right next to her.

"At this moment, I don't know exactly," Tiffany said. "What's wrong?"

"I'll tell you what's wrong," Whitley said. "I told that woman I needed access to the water line for my space. The hose has been removed again and rerouted to her hot yoga tent across the way."

"Are you sure?" Billie stepped across the road to see for herself. The woman was correct. The fresh water supply was behind the yoga tent. Another quick check of her notes revealed that Kelly had not requested access to fresh water on her site.

"How do you know it was Kelly?" Tiffany asked.

"Did you remove it and place it over there?" Whitley demanded.

"No." Tiffany shook her head. "But I haven't seen Kelly in more than an hour. I was just about to look for her."

"I'll check the yoga tent," Billie volunteered, wanting to get away. She searched for a moment for the entrance. Unlike the other tents around it, the flap opening was not in the front. She had to turn sideways between the yoga tent and the one set up next to it just to get inside. "Kelly?" she called the woman's name as she entered. The moment she'd moved the flap she could feel the humidity from the tent on her face. It was like a sauna at the gym, only much more intense.

The interior of the tent was dim with only a couple of pink salt lamps illuminating the space. Long, colored sheers hung from the center of the tent and stretched out in a circle. In the dim light, the tent had a purplish hue cast against the canvas walls. "Kelly," Billie called out again.

"Nothing over here," Tiffany shouted from across the road. Billie moved slowly toward a pile of pillows in the far corner of the tent. She stepped carefully across the damp floor. As she walked, she realized there was probably a no shoes allowed policy inside the tent. She would have to double check and make sure her shoes had not left any dirt or mud behind when she got the chance.

Something felt off about the pillows in the corner. Billie pulled her phone out of her pocket and turned on her flashlight. As soon as she did, the shape of the woman lying on the floor struck her. She gasped and stepped closer. "Kelly? Are you alright? Kelly!"

"What's the matter?" Tiffany called from outside of the tent.

"We need an ambulance," Billie shouted. "And help me turn the lights on in here if there are any." A second later, Tiffany burst through the tent flap and flipped on an overhead lamp Billie had not noticed before. She bent over the woman and strained to get a closer look. "I don't want to move her, but it looks like she is not with us any longer." Her words came out more gently than she'd expected. Inside her mind reeled from the sight.

Kelly Peck's body was oddly twisted. Her face was red, and her lips were blue. Parts of her long, layered skirt appeared to be twisted around her feet.

Billie winced as Tiffany stepped closer and filled the tent with an ear-piercing scream. As soon as she was finished, Billie turned her phone over in her hand and began dialing Detective Sullivan.

## CHAPTER 4

"Why on earth is it so hot in here?" Sully complained as she held the large camera over the pile of pillows and the body of the woman lying among them. She snapped a dozen or so pictures in rapid succession, then moved around the tent for a different angle.

"Hot yoga," Billie said from the entrance. "They make the room really, really hot and work out."

"But, why? That sounds terrible," Sully said, standing up straight. She shook her head and resumed looking over the body. "We won't know until the coroner shows up for her, but there doesn't appear to be any visible sign of trauma or injury. Can you open that tent flap a little more? And for crying out loud, can you find out how we turn off that heater thing?"

"It's like a sauna or something, I think," Billie said, still feeling dizzy from the heat and humidity herself. "I think you just have to stop pouring water over it."

"Well, someone must have melted a glacier over it," Sully said. "Look at the sides. Water is pooling and collecting from the condensation."

"It is really hot," Billie said. Maybe it was the fact that they were already on an island in the Gulf of Mexico, but she had never been in a sauna quite that hot before. Then again, hot yoga was hardly her thing.

She inhaled three deep breaths of air and opened the tent flap even more, knowing a blast of heat was going to get her again. She secured the flap as far as she could with the pen she had found on the ground in front of it and let in more fresh air for Sully.

"Thank you," Sully groaned. "Any chance you have something cold to drink handy? I don't think I can do this much longer without a gallon of ice water."

Billie nodded and stepped away from the tent. She looked around at the small crowd of vendors that had gathered around and shook her head. She would have to push her way through them and hope that no one stopped her and demanded answers she didn't have to give.

"Billie! Hey, Billie," Rhonda shouted from the back of the crowd behind her. Billie turned and smiled at the familiar face. "Hey, can I help with anything?"

"Ice water," Billie yelled back. "Anything cold to drink will do."

"On it," Rhonda said. She took off toward the commissary kitchen.

Billie spotted the police chief making his way through the crowd. "Chief Abernathy," she said when he made his way over to her. "I have Rhonda going after cold drinks. I think your team is going to need them."

"What happened?" the chief asked her quietly. "In your own words, of course. And why are all of these people ogling?"

Billie shook her head. "There was a disagreement between the victim and another vendor over which space belonged to whom," she explained in a whisper. "We sorted it out, but I wanted to return this morning to make sure everything was fine with both parties. When I went to look for Kelly, I couldn't find her at first. Her business partner, Tiffany, was looking for her as well. Anyway, I looked inside this tent and found her on a pile of pillows in the corner."

"This is where they have a sauna and a yoga class at the same time?" Chief Abernathy asked.

Billie nodded. "That's why Kelly wanted two adjoining sites, but she didn't make that clear to Asher. She signed off on the two he showed her."

The chief went inside the tent and chatted with Sully for a moment. He poked his head out and gestured to Billie. They stood just outside the open tent flap. "Was there a class scheduled for this morning?" he asked. "I thought the fair was supposed to begin tomorrow."

"It is," Billie said. "I don't have anything scheduled for any vendor until first thing in the morning."

"Maybe they were doing a dry run," Sully suggested when she came out for air. "Or in this case, a damp run, I suppose."

Billie shook her head. "Normally, they let us know what they plan to do before they do it," she replied. "I don't have anything from the vendor indicating that they intended to run the sauna at this time."

"I don't know what she was doing," Tiffany called from a few feet away.

"Who is that?" the chief whispered.

"That's Tiffany Bonner, Chief," Sully said loudly. "She's the business partner."

"And who did the deceased have a disagreement with yesterday?" he asked Billie.

"Whitley Carson," Billie said. She found the woman's name and information on the diagram she'd folded and shoved in her pocket and pointed it out to the chief.

"Much of this is very new to me," he said. "I won't pretend to know anything about all of this holistic stuff, but if someone can point me in her direction, I'll go and talk to her."

"She's over this way," Billie said, directing the chief to the tent across the way.

Chief Abernathy nodded once and headed into the other tent. He announced himself with a "knock-knock" and pushed the flap to the side. Billie waited for a second, then headed back toward the hot tent.

"Do you need me for anything else?" she asked Sully.

"Just that cold water you promised me," Sully replied.

Billie looked out over the crowd again. She spotted Rhonda walking toward her with a large, soft-sided cooler. "Give me just a second."

"Excuse me," Rhonda said as she made her way through the crowd. "Man, these people don't want to move out of the way."

"I don't know what they're waiting around hoping to see," Billie whispered to her when she made her way over. "Thank you, by the way. You're a lifesaver."

"I think I'm actually a little too late for that," Rhonda said.

"So was I, apparently," Billie said. She took the cooler from Rhonda and headed back to the tent where Sully stood, making notes. Billie opened the cooler and found it full of water bottles, various juices, teas, and other choices. "Rhonda came through in a big way. Do you want water, juice, tea, or a soda?"

Sully looked up. "Mountain Dew? Don't judge me. I know water would hydrate me more, but I could use the caffeine."

Billie nodded and pulled out a bottle for her. "Here you are," she said when Sully came out to get it. "Do you plan to be here for a while?"

Sully opened the bottle and drank down quite a bit. "I'm afraid so," she said. "Though I do hope most of the heat will be out of here before long. I'm waiting for the coroner's office to show up and do what they need to do."

"I'll leave this here for you, then," Billie said.

"That is, if it's okay for me to head back to the kitchen."

"You can go," she said. "I have a statement from you and the other witnesses. Do me a favor and don't discuss your statement with any of the other witnesses, though. I know you're going to talk to Rhonda about it, but please, be careful what you say."

Billie chuckled. "I'm just going to head back to the commissary kitchen and call Asher," she said. "We have to determine whether or not to go ahead with the fair."

"I'll talk to the chief and get him to make his recommendation soon," Sully said as Billie was walking away.

"Hey," Rhonda said, standing a few feet away.

"I'm leaving the cooler here with Sully," Billie said. "I hope that's okay."

"No problem. Are you staying here too?"

Billie shook her head. "No, I need to go back and grab something to eat," she said.

"Why don't we go down to the boardwalk and grab ourselves a vegan snack?" Rhonda suggested. "I saw some of the trucks were already open for business when I walked over. And you know me, a promise is a promise."

Billie smiled. "That sounds like a plan," she said. "I am pretty hungry."

"Me too," Rhonda said. "I woke up this morning and decided that if I was ever going to try a vegan burger, today would be the day." She hooked her arm in Billie's and guided her gently through the crowd.

# CHAPTER 5

"Good morning, ladies," Toren said when they approached the truck. He turned to flip a few patties on the hot griddle behind him. Billie smiled at the design of the exterior. She had chosen a green background with bright white letters. Unlike many of the other truck managers, Toren had chosen to come to the island weeks before the truck was ready.

He toured the workshop where Nolan Wiggins worked on the inside of the truck, even before he had confirmation that the job was his. He weighed in with his opinion on the interior placement of the grills and the wide griddle and consulted with Nolan when he chose the refrigerator and truck-size walk-in cooler that took up the back of the truck.

Billie made her mind up rather quickly when she

watched his interaction with Nolan discussing the exterior of the truck. He campaigned for a sleek background for the top two-thirds of the truck and drew out his vision of a bright green back one-third separated by a thick, angled blue line. Instead of a large truck name, he designed two word clouds, one just behind the cab of the truck with various fonts in bright green and a smaller cloud in black font on the back.

The result was a smart, sleek look with all the information the customer needed in each of the word clouds. The large cloud was filled with words like "vegan burger, chicken sandwich, plant-based, shiitake mushroom, onions," and so on. Most of the words were taken directly from the illuminated menu board that appeared when the awning window was raised.

While the larger word cloud answered the "what" about the truck, the smaller word cloud spoke to "why." Billie scanned the words in the cloud and smiled. Toren had a clever way to push the vegan lifestyle with humor. His suggestions included "eat plants, not faces" and "vegetables deserve death" along with "vegans live longer" and "don't clog my heart." The result was eye-catching and conversation starting.

"I feel like I need to call my cardiologist and apologize." Rhonda chuckled as she read the second word cloud.

"Okay, what can I get you?" Toren asked when he returned to the window.

"One of each," Rhonda said. "I mean, do you have a sampler platter or something?"

"I have an idea," Billie spoke up. "Why don't we get a couple of sliders and a charcuterie board."

"Sounds great," Toren agreed.

"I want to try the tacos as well," Rhonda said.

Toren nodded and pointed toward the glass-front cooler in the back. "Wait here while I grab a board for the two of you. I'll get you started with that and call you when the hot food is ready."

"We're going to grab a seat at the picnic tables right over there," Billie said. She accepted the board from Toren and walked toward the picnic tables ahead of Rhonda.

"Hey, boss lady," Dillon whispered to her from his truck. He winked and handed over two drinks. Dillon liked to prepare cherry coke when she was on the boardwalk. If Rhonda was with her, he doubled her order.

"Thank you, Dillon," Rhonda sang out. They took their seats across from each other. Billie pulled the heavy cellophane back from the board and plucked a grape from the center.

"This is interesting," Rhonda said. "Is this wood?"

"Aren't they cool? They're made out of bamboo."

Rhonda looked sideways at her. "Isn't bamboo wood?"

Billie chuckled. "Actually, bamboo is a grass, like a reed," she said. "You see what this job does to me?"

"Makes you a walking encyclopedia filled with trivia and random information?"

"Precisely," Billie said. She picked up a piece of vegan cheese and took a bite.

"How is it?" Rhonda asked her hesitantly.

"Not bad," Billie said. "The texture is a little different, but the taste is excellent. You can't tell that it isn't cut right from a block of genuine sharp cheddar cheese."

"What is it made of, though?" Rhonda asked. "Do I even want to know?"

"I think most of what Toren chose for the menu is fairly natural," Billie said. "This is made out of peas and soybeans."

"Okay, ladies," Toren called from the window. Billie stood up and headed toward the food truck. She turned back and jerked her head toward Rhonda. Toren set out several platters, all on recycled, biodegradable trays, filled with several sliders, a half-dozen tacos, nachos, and a variety of crepes.

"Holy cow," Rhonda said.

"Actually, 'holy beans' is more accurate," Toren remarked with his best poker face. Billie chuckled and picked up the nachos and tacos.

"Thank you." Billie beamed. She planned to set aside a large tip for him when she returned to the kitchen.

Rhonda followed her back to the table with the sliders in one hand and the crepes in the other. "I don't even know where to start," she said.

"I do," Billie said and plucked a slider off of the stack. She bit into the burger and waited while the tastes filled her mouth. "Whoa."

"Whoa?" Rhonda asked.

Billie nodded and popped the rest of the slider into her mouth. "It's like a burger, but more than a burger," she said. "I mean, the consistency is very burger-like, and the smoky taste is amazing, but it's almost like he made a real beef patty and grilled it up on a bed of roasted vegetables."

Rhonda eagerly bit into a burger and nodded her head. "Oh, my gosh," she said around a mouth filled with the slider. "You're right! This is amazing. Amazing, Toren!" she shouted down the boardwalk.

"Thank you, Miss Rhonda," Toren called back to her.

"Nachos next," Rhonda said. She picked up a chip and shoved it into the layered dip. Billie followed suit. She dunked her chip into the vegan beef, refried beans, nacho cheese, and sour cream. Rhonda smiled and went for more.

Billie sampled everything but sat back, stuffed full while Rhonda continued to indulge. She smiled and commented with nearly every bite. "I take it you are a vegan convert now," she said to her friend.

Rhonda nodded and held up her index finger while she finished the last bite. "I'm not giving up meat, but I think I could go for a vegan meal once or twice a week."

"I think I can agree with that," Billie said. She stood up after they were done and began gathering up the trash for the waste bin while Rhonda practically licked her fingers clean. "I have to get back to the kitchen."

Rhonda nodded. "Do you think the Holistic Fair will end up getting canceled?"

Billie shrugged. "I honestly don't know," she said. Her phone buzzed inside her back pocket. She pulled it out and looked at the screen. "I'm about to find out, I guess. It's Asher. I'd better take this." She waved to

Rhonda and turned to head back toward the festival grounds with the phone at her ear.

"Sounds like you've had an exciting day," Asher said on the other end.

"Yeah, you can say that again," Billie said.

"Are they calling it a homicide?" Asher asked.

"I think that's what Sully said earlier," Billie said. "I don't know how to describe what was going on in that tent, but the woman who died, Kelly, she wore this skirt that had like 20 layers to it, and some parts of the fabric were sort of wound around her feet when I found her."

"What about you? Are you doing okay?"

"Yeah," Billie said numbly. "I wish you were here."

"I'm thinking about heading back early," Asher said.

"No, don't cut your time short with your family," Billie said, "By the way, how did you even find out about everything?"

"Dillon called me as soon as he heard," Asher said. "There's a reason that guy is in charge when we're gone."

"That and the fact that he always has a soda ready for me whenever I'm down on the boardwalk," Billie said.

"Are you there now?" Asher asked.

"Just left," Billie said. "Rhonda had to try out the vegan truck."

"What did she think?" Asher asked with a chuckle.

"Well, she decided the food is delicious, but she isn't quite ready to give up meat," Billie said. "The food is really good. You would be really shocked how good those burgers are."

Billie ended the phone call after she made Asher promise not to cut his visit short. There was no way she wanted to take him away from his family.

## CHAPTER 6

Billie returned to the kitchen and headed straight for Asher's office. She placed the diagram of the fair on his desk and sat down. What she wanted was word one way or the other about the fate of the fair. The Holistic Fair was one of the larger festivals of the year and a big moneymaker for them. Billie wanted to see it through. This was, after all, the first real shot she had to show Asher that she could run things by herself.

Of course, Billie understood the gravity of the situation. A woman had been found dead in one of the large tents on the festival grounds. All signs pointed to murder, and the killer could very easily still be walking around among the other vendors.

Billie looked over the map of the festival grounds

again. She read through the names of the vendors listed on the diagram. There were over a hundred separate vendors booked for the four-day event. The fair organizers had a list of requirements for the participating vendors, although Billie wasn't exactly sure what was included, she knew from the event description that everything sold there had to pass some sort of holistic sniff test.

Most of the vendors either sold herbs or other natural remedies, offered yoga or meditation services, or hawked products based on one form of New Age spirituality or the other. There were candle sellers and essential oil dealers. Some claimed the wisdom of ancient shamans and Native American medicine men.

No matter how she might have felt about the vendors, thousands of people were expected for the fair. That wasn't something to take lightly.

Billie left Asher's office and headed to her own. Toren had signed his truck manager contract immediately after accepting the job. Billie was beyond impressed with his professionalism. He was young, but anything he might have lacked in experience he made up with the determination to successfully run the food truck. She flipped her light on and pulled her desk chair out. She took a seat in front of her desk and opened up her work computer, then sat and stared at the screen for five straight minutes.

She had no idea what she was supposed to be doing at that moment in time. And the last thing she wanted to do was admit it, especially to Asher. For over two years, she had followed him around the commissary kitchen and the festival grounds paying very little attention to what he actually did day in and day out. She had a general idea, but it seemed like most of their focus had been on her food trucks and her truck managers, not necessarily on the daily ins and outs of running a successful fair.

In fact, Asher was so good at his job, that not one of the organizers had been to her with a single question. She had dealt with the issue between Kelly and Whitley herself, but she honestly couldn't say if that had been the right way to handle it. It was certainly the most direct way to deal with it, but for all she knew she had violated some sort of etiquette or proper procedure.

Maybe what she needed to do was to check in with the fair organizers themselves. She stood up then sat right back down. What if they wanted answers about the murder? She had no answers yet. What if they demanded an answer right then and there about whether the fair would continue as scheduled or not?

Billie moved her laptop and folded her arms and laid her head down on the desk. She fought the temptation to bang her head on it repeatedly. Who knew her words to Asher would come back to haunt her so quickly?

"I can take care of a fair, babe," she had said. "No problem! No worries! I've seen you do it a hundred times! I know what I am doing."

But she did not know what she was doing, and it didn't take a genius to figure that out. She rose up and rubbed her eyes. What was that saying? Her last boss in Boston had said it constantly when she worked at the last greasy spoon before Alex Regent had called her to fill her in on the large inheritance she had received from her late grandmother, Adeline.

"Fake it until you make it," she repeated out loud. "Time to fake it." Billie pushed herself back in the chair and stood up. She inhaled deeply and picked up her phone from her desk. As soon as her hands were on it, the phone rang. The ringing shocked her, but she gathered her wits and picked it up before the call went to voicemail.

"Billie?" The voice on the other end spoke before she knew who she was speaking to.

"Yeah," Billie said. "Hi, Sully."

"I was just calling to tell you that the chief doesn't

plan to request that the fair shut down," Sully said. "We've collected all the necessary evidence and cleared the crime scene, but we are going to increase police presence. The sheriff's department is sending some deputies over to help us out."

"Wow," Billie said, realizing that it was officially a homicide now. "The fair will be crawling with law enforcement."

"Is there a problem with that?" Sully asked.

"Oh, not at all," Billie said. "I'm glad so many will be around. Hopefully nothing else happens."

"It's likely there will be some looky-loos showing up," Sully continued. "Once word gets out about the murder."

"I figured as much," Billie said. "I'm going right now to meet with the organizers and see what they have to say about all of this."

"I spoke with one of them already," Sully told her. "He's pretty worked up about all of this."

"Is he?" Billie scanned the flier on her desk advertising the fair. Of course, she had no memory of the organizers' names off the top of her head.

"Yeah, he said he wanted to shut things down, but the other two on the committee with him voted to remain open," Sully said. "Pending what law enforcement decided, of course."

"Jamison," Billie said out loud as soon as she spotted the names on the back of the flier. "Hector Jamison. That's who you spoke with."

"Was that a question?" Sully asked.

"Yeah. No," Billie said quickly. "I just want to make sure no one is trying to pull a fast one on us." She rolled her eyes at herself. Way to cover up the fact that she was terribly unprepared for this conversation.

"Why would someone try to pull a fast one on us?" Sully asked. Ever the sharp-witted detective.

"Why would someone commit murder a day before the fair opens? We have no idea who we're dealing with here," Billie said, then promptly held her breath and hoped that the response was a decent one.

"Well, that is true," Sully said. Billie sighed in relief. "You go on and meet with the organizers, but you let me know if you get a weird vibe from any of them."

"Yes, of course," Billie said. She studied the names on the flier. Hector Jamison, Tara Kingscourt, and Myrtle Wilder. Maybe one of them knew something about the killer. There was only one way to find out.

## CHAPTER 7

"Are murders something that happen around here often?" Myrtle Wilder asked Billie when she took a seat. They were outside near the large outdoor yoga studio that had been set up in the midway of the festival grounds. Carnival rides were typically set up in the area, but the place had been transformed. Large potted trees had been brought in and realistic-looking synthetic grass covered the asphalt. Large sections of the fake grass were covered with dozens of cushy yoga mats, and rows of white chairs surrounded the grassy area.

"Like any tourist island, we have our share of crime," Billie said. She did her best to remain composed while she spoke to the fair organizers, but their questions over the past ten minutes had her yearning for the privacy and isolation of her tiny house.

"And remind me, Ms. Halifax, where is Mr. Scanlan exactly?" Tara Kingscourt asked her with the air of English nobility. Billie half expected to see her raise a pinky as she spoke.

"As I explained before, Asher is visiting family," Billie said.

"Well, was there a death in his family or some other emergency?" Tara asked her.

"I don't think that is really any of our business," Hector Jamison replied. He was the oldest of the three, though his manners and kind eyes made Billie think of a much younger man when he spoke. Myrtle and Tara were the ones acting like aged curmudgeons.

"It most certainly is our business," Myrtle protested. "I would like to know why the owner of this place would elect to leave at the exact time this fair was set to occur. One would think that such a large fair might be important enough for him to stick around. How very unprofessional."

Billie swallowed hard before she spoke. Despite her concern about the fair, her patience was starting to wear thin. "Mr. Scanlan is the co-owner here," she said. "I am the other owner, and I can assure you that we both have your concerns in mind. If you prefer, we can cancel the fair with or without law enforcement's approval."

"We've been through this already. No one is suggesting that we shut everything down," Tara said. "We would just feel better if Mr. Scanlan was present to handle things."

"What things would you like handled, exactly?" Billie asked. "If you prefer to remain open, nothing much has changed from the way things were going before Kelly was killed. I've left the door wide open to the police. As a matter of fact, it was me who called them in the first place."

"And how exactly did that happen?" Myrtle asked her. "Why were you there?"

"Because there was an issue between two vendors about who had rented which space," Billie said. "I dealt with it right away when I arrived with the paperwork to settle the dispute. My presence when the body was discovered was the result of me checking in on things."

"Why weren't we consulted?" Myrtle asked. "That should have been handled by the three of us."

"I'm curious about that myself," Hector said.

"Did any of you have the diagram and map of the festival grounds? Aside from what we provided you with originally," Billie said. "Did you have access to the communication between the vendors and Asher? I did, and I did my best to quickly settle the matter."

"It was an internal situation," Tara insisted. "You should have come to us when one of our vendors had an issue with another one."

"You didn't book their spaces," Billie said. "Your vendors booked directly with us. I doubt you would have even raised the issue if the body hadn't been discovered."

"What are you trying to say?" Myrtle demanded.

"I'm just saying that you only have an issue after the fact," Billie said. "Otherwise, you would have opted to organize the vendors yourselves instead of leaving that to us. We offer that as an option, you know. You should have been told that when you set the fair up." Maybe she knew more about this business than she gave herself credit for.

"Yes, well, that puts us in a precarious spot," Myrtle said. "We set things up this way because it takes some of the work off of our shoulders."

"Let's be honest," Hector cut in. "Letting the vendors set up directly with the festival grounds company saves us the headache of getting the bills paid. We skip that step for a reason."

"And that is perfectly reasonable," Billie said.

"That's why we offer that option, but along with that, it does give us some control when there are disputes."

"I can't help feeling like we missed something this time," Tara said. "Maybe if we had done things differently, we might have seen an issue before someone got killed."

"We've had problems before and that didn't stop anything," Hector muttered.

"Pardon me," Billie interrupted. "You have had problems before? What are you talking about?"

Tara stood up suddenly. "I think our time here is over, Ms. Halifax," she said. "We all have things to do before the fair opens tomorrow."

"Hold on a moment," Billie said. "If you've had issues before with this fair, especially with known participants or vendors, you have to share that information with me. I think that would be important for us to know about."

"Thank you for your time, Billie," Myrtle said. She stood up as well.

Billie inhaled a deep breath and forced herself to slowly exhale. "Look, there is a clause in your contract that requires you to divulge any information pertinent to public safety. That much I know. If there is something going on here that I need to know about, that may have a bearing on whether this fair should go forward or not, I think you should tell me right now."

"Is that a threat, Ms. Halifax?" Myrtle asked.

Billie shook her head. "Of course not," she said. "But if there is something you know about that poses a threat to my staff or the vendors or anyone else, you have a moral and a contractual duty to report it."

"Duly noted," Tara said. "Now, if you will excuse us, please."

Billie nodded her head, deciding to let it go for now. "Alright. I'll be around if you need anything."

"Ms. Halifax," Myrtle said before Billie turned to walk away. "I do hope that you will not run to the police and try to cause more trouble. We will sue you for, well, I don't know what, but we'll find something. Based on what I see here, you have a lot to lose."

Billie glanced at Hector Jamison. He turned his head away as soon as she looked at him.

"Duly noted," Billie said wryly and walked away. She headed straight back to the commissary kitchen and poured herself a cup of coffee from the kitchen and returned directly to her office. She pulled her phone out and stared at it for a moment, tempted to call Asher and ask for his advice.

She wasn't ready quite yet to admit defeat, so

instead, she rushed back down the hallway to Asher's office. She opened the top drawer of his filing cabinet and fished out the contract he had for the Holistic Fair. She scanned the contract and found the exact clause she had mentioned. "Man, I am better at this than I thought," she said. She returned the contract back to the folder and shut the drawer.

She headed back down the hall to her own office with a copy of the map from Asher's desk. It was crystal clear to her that the organizers wanted her to keep far away from their fair, but she had a real interest in finding out if there were more issues to come. Nothing was going to stop her now.

## CHAPTER 8

The afternoon sun shone bright overhead when Billie left the commissary kitchen again. She carried a folded copy of the fair diagram with her as she walked. The wind had picked up considerably. She could smell the salty air in the breeze. It was her favorite type of afternoon. Since coming to the island, she had grown to love the breezes off of the gulf on sunny afternoons. It was a near-perfect day.

She walked toward the entrance and nodded at the sheriff's deputies that had already arrived to keep an eye on the fair. The coroner's team had packed up and left a couple of hours before. Billie was grateful to see that the area where the poor woman had been killed was back to normal. She was surprised to see that both tents were still up. Surely Kelly's partner wasn't planning to carry on with the fair, she thought.

Billie decided to steer clear of the area for the time being. She was more interested in getting a feel for the other vendors before the fair began in the morning. Something the organizers had said to her when she met with them earlier still bothered her. What sort of problem had they experienced before? It seemed ridiculous to think it, but could there be some sort of holistic fair serial killer roaming around?

What was more likely, was that there were some strange issues among the members. While Billie had zero idea where the investigation stood, she wondered if Sully and the chief had questioned Whitley just yet. It seemed to Billie that she would be the most logical person to start with.

But there was also Tiffany, Kelly's business partner. Maybe the two of them were in some sort of disagreement. The truth was, Billie had very little information to go on. In fact, she wasn't entirely sure how the woman had died in the first place. What she did know was that layers of the woman's skirt were wrapped around her ankles, and that her skin had been discolored. The only thing she was sure of was that her death had taken place in a hot tent with enough humidity to cause puddles to form on the floor.

She looked up to see Sully a few yards ahead of her, walking directly toward her. "Are you busy?" Sully asked her when they met up.

"I was just walking around looking over everything before the fair opens in the morning," Billie said. "What's going on?"

"Walk with me," Sully said. She turned Billie around and headed back toward the entrance.

"What's going on?" Billie asked her.

"I need to know everything you know about this fair," Sully said in hushed tones.

"Of course," Billie said. "What do you need to know?"

"Absolutely anything you can tell me," Sully whispered. "I have no idea how to talk to these people. I ask them a question, and all I get is some mystical woo-woo answer." She shuddered as she spoke.

"Mystical woo-woo answer? Like what?"

Sully stopped her in the middle of the walkway. "Like, I asked one of these people about the other people in the fair, you know, what does she know about her fellow vendors. That sort of thing," Sully said.

"That sounds like a reasonable question," Billie said.

"Yeah, well, too bad she couldn't just give me a reasonable answer in return," the detective said. "She starts running on about how we are all caught in some cosmic web trying to spin ourselves free of our suffering."

"That didn't do much to answer your question." Billie chuckled.

"You're telling me! All I wanted to know was whether or not she knew if there was any conflict among the vendors, anything that might shed light on the murder," Sully continued. "You know what I got for an answer that time? She started going on and on about how conflict is just a manifestation of our inner turmoil. I swear she told me we were living in some sort of simulation of our own creation."

"Sounds like she was trying to evade your questions," Billie said bluntly.

Sully nodded. "You might be right about her being evasive."

"Maybe you should try to talk to more people," Billie suggested.

"Like who?"

"Well." Billie looked around. "Why not start with those people over there selling organic soaps? They might be less apt to be so mystical and woo-woo, as you put it."

"Okay, good plan," Sully said. "Let's go." She grabbed Billie by the arm and pulled her along toward the exit to the festival grounds.

"Wait, you want me to go with you?" Billie asked.

"You can help me break the ice, I suppose," Sully said. "Do you have some sort of map of this place? I want to talk to a few hand-selected people before I run into another one like whatever that woman was back there."

Billie pulled the diagram out of her pocket. "I have this," she said and handed it over to Sully.

"Perfect," Sully said. She carried the diagram with her as she walked. She looked up in time to smile at the organic soap vendor, a gray-headed man dressed in a loose denim shirt and khakis. "You talk first. I might intimidate him." She nudged Billie as they slowed their pace.

Billie swiped the diagram from Sully for a moment and looked up the vendor's name. "Good afternoon, Mr. Healy," she said. "Are you all ready for tomorrow?"

"I'm almost there." Mr. Healy smiled at her and nodded to Sully. "Afternoon, Detective."

Billie could feel Sully stiffen behind her. "How did you know?" Sully asked.

"You're not very subtle," the older man admitted. "But I have no problem with you stopping by. Why don't you step inside, and we can talk." He led them under a large canopy. Unlike many of the other vendors, he used an open air tent for his display. Billie wondered if it had to do with the fragrant nature of the items he sold. Even in the breeze, she could smell the pungent odor of many of the soaps.

"I wanted to know if you had any idea who might have wanted to hurt Kelly Peck?" Sully asked him. "I know that's a pretty forward question, but I'm trying to narrow down a list of suspects and so far, I don't have much." Billie was taken back by the detective's blunt admission.

Mr. Healy nodded his head. "Unfortunately, this is my first time at one of these events," he said. "I wish I could be of some help to you, but I honestly don't know anything about any of the people here."

"Understood," Sully said. "I appreciate you answering me in plain English like that."

"Pardon me?"

"She's run into a few creative answers to her questions," Billie explained.

"Ah, I see." Mr. Healy chuckled. "If there is

anything else I can help you with, please let me know."

"Actually, do you have any products for animals?" Billie asked. "I have a Tibetan Mastiff who really enjoys soaking in salt water."

"I have just the thing," Mr. Healy said. He walked to a basket filled with hand cut bar soaps on the far side of the tent. "This is safe for human use, as well. It's made from goat's milk and cocoa butter. You lather that up when you bathe your dog and I guarantee his coat will shine like never before."

"Wonderful." Billie beamed. "Thank you. What do I owe you?"

Mr. Healy grinned. "It's on the house," he said. "I give out samples all the time."

Billie thanked him again and turned the bar over in her hand to read more of the ingredients. "Tell me something," she said casually. "Have you ever heard of any problems with holistic fairs like this before? Maybe not murders, but any fighting or anything?"

Mr. Healy's grin faded. He looked around and nodded slowly. "Some of my fellow soap makers warned me against coming to larger fairs like this," he said. "I don't know any details, but he said some of these vendors can really start trouble with each other, something like girls fighting in middle school."

"Oh, that sounds awful," Sully said. "But you haven't seen anything like that yourself, have you?"

Mr. Healy shook his head. "I promised my wife that if I did, I would just pack up and go home. I'm here to sell my products and meet people interested in organic soaps, and that's all."

Sully thanked him for his time and led Billie back out of his tent. "See? That's why I need you with me. You're so down to earth. Asking about dog soap was a genius way to make him feel more comfortable."

"Thanks, but that was for real. Waffles really did need something." She shrugged. "I'm curious, have you questioned Whitley or Tiffany yet?"

Sully nodded. "I have, and their answers were as predictable as you can imagine. I don't think there's much more to know about either of them."

Billie said nothing as they walked around the next half-dozen or so vendors. She introduced herself to about ten new faces and asked a couple of questions before Sully jumped in with her more direct queries. None of the conversations yielded anything of substance.

"Billie! Billie, can you come back to the kitchen?" She turned around to find Isa running after her.

"What's wrong?" Billie asked as soon as she caught up with her.

"Hot water heater," Isa said. "One of them is spewing water."

"Oh, you have got to be kidding," Billie said. "Sully-"

"Go, go," Sully said, waving her hand. "Call your maintenance guy and get this handled. I'll catch up with you later on."

# CHAPTER 9

Billie waited in her office while the maintenance team and the plumber they hired from the mainland worked. As it turned out, there was an issue with the pipes as well. Once again, she rested her head on her desk and wished Asher was there to handle things.

"Heard you're having some issues," Dillon said from her doorway. Billie raised her head and nodded.

"You heard correctly," she said, gesturing for him to come inside and close the door. "Please tell me you're not here with another problem."

Dillon smiled. "I'm not," he said. "I just wandered over to check on you. Isa informed everyone about what was going on."

Billie pushed herself back from her desk and

stood up. "She said she was here to grab something she had forgotten in the cooler when she heard the water hissing from the utility room," she said.

Dillon nodded. "Olivia covered for Isa. I was starting to get worried when she was gone for more than ten minutes. It usually doesn't take that long for a truck manager to run back here after something."

Billie stared at him for a moment. "Does Olivia do that often? Watch someone's truck for them while they run errands?" It was the first she had heard of her truck managers covering for each other.

"Yeah, well, Olivia has the ability to run back and forth without leaving a truck unmanned," he said.

"We've all learned to cover for each other. In fact, I think she could be a sous chef for a few of them. She's had enough experience. Of course, she's taking care of my truck at the moment."

"While you're back here checking on me," Billie said.

"Don't be angry at me for that," Dillon said. He shrugged his shoulders. "Asher asked me to keep an eye out while he's out of town."

Billie smiled. "We both trust you to handle things if we're away, Dillon," she said. "And I know he trusts you to look out for me, too. There's nothing I could get angry over."

"Well, it's a relief to hear you think that way," Dillon said. "You're very capable. Nobody doubts that at all, but there's a lot to manage here. You always have a full plate as it is with the trucks, but this week you have the fair as well. Not to mention the fact that one of the vendors was killed."

Billie nodded toward her desk. "That's the main reason you found me with my head down," she said. "I hope we're doing the right thing, keeping everything open."

"Didn't the police make that call?" Dillon asked.

"They made that recommendation," Billie said. "My understanding is, unless there's a compelling reason to, they prefer not to shut things down."

"I can see why," Dillon said. "With this many people on the island at once, shutting things down is bound to cause more harm than good."

"That's basically what Sully and the chief said, too," Billie agreed. "I just wish I knew what to think about all of this. I met with the three-person committee earlier, and that did nothing to inspire my confidence."

"That doesn't sound very promising," he said. "Care to elaborate?"

"It wasn't anything specific. We were discussing the fact that I dealt with the conflict between Kelly and another vendor before Kelly wound up dead. The three organizers were not happy that I took the initiative to deal with things," Billie said. "One of them, Hector, referred to problems they have run into before. When I tried to ask more questions, the meeting ended pretty fast."

"Almost as if there was something they didn't want you to know," Dillon said.

"Exactly like that," Billie said. "And the thing is, we have a clause in our contract that requires them to disclose anything that could pose a threat to the public."

"And they are aware of this?"

Billie nodded. "Yes, and that should make me feel a little better than it does."

"Maybe you should do some looking into things," Dillon suggested. "If it was anything too wild, I bet there's been some sort of news coverage about it."

"True," Billie agreed. "It shouldn't be too hard to find out whether or not these guys were involved."

Dillon opened his mouth to speak but stopped when the door burst open, and a small group of vendors rushed inside. Billie wasn't on a first name basis with any of them, but she did recognize a few from her conversations with Sully.

"Miss Halifax!" One of the younger women

moved toward her. "The cops just arrested Tiffany Bonner!"

Billie glanced at Dillon. "Slow down," she said to the young woman. "Are you sure?"

"Yes! We just watched that detective friend of yours put her in handcuffs and lead her away."

"Well, that was fast," Dillon said. He nodded to Billie and headed back to the utility room.

"Why don't we all go back to my office?" Billie suggested to the small group. "We have an issue going on here with the hot water heaters and pipes." She led them back to her office and listened for more than fifteen minutes as they spoke over each other to express their concerns.

When she could finally get a word in, Billie offered each one a generic gift certificate for a visit to the boardwalk and their food truck of choice. When she ushered them back out of the building at last, she picked up her phone and called Sully immediately.

"I had a feeling you would be calling me," Sully said when she answered the phone.

"What's going on?" Billie asked. "You just made an arrest?"

"I can't go into too much detail at the moment, but yes, she has been arrested," Sully said.

"Where is Tiffany now?" Billie asked.

"She is being taken to the mainland to the county jail," Sully said.

## CHAPTER 10

"We're going to have to shut the water off for a little while," Dillon informed Billie ten minutes later.

Her mind still reeled from the news that the partner of the victim had been arrested for murder.

"And why is the water going to be shut off?"

"So, they can replace the water heater and fix the trouble with the pipe. Have you forgotten?" He laughed. "You're pretty preoccupied at the moment, huh?"

"I'm sorry," Billie said. "My mind is going in a hundred different directions."

"I get it," Dillon said. "At least an arrest was made. That has to be a relief."

"It really is a relief," Billie said. "The timing for shutting the water off isn't great, but at least it's not happening first thing in the morning when you guys are going to need all of the water you can get while you prep for the day."

"Why don't you wait right here while I go and let them know that we're good with shutting the water off?" Dillon said.

"Hold on," Billie said. Her brain had finally begun to process what he'd told her. "Are you saying the water will be shut off to the entire area or just this building?"

Dillon smiled. "Just to the building," he said. "And possibly to your house and Polly's, too."

"I'm sure Polly will appreciate that."

"She can always go to her sister's apartment if she needs to," Dillon said.

"I can go to Asher's houseboat, if I have to," Billie said. "Although I can't tell you how Waffles is going to feel about that."

"He'll love the adventure, I'm sure."

"You're probably right," Billie said. "By the way, Dillon, I can't thank you enough for all of your help dealing with this plumbing issue."

"That's what I'm here for. It's no trouble at all," he assured her. "What are you going to do for the rest of the day?"

"Well, I think I'm going to make the rounds again

before I retire for the night," she said. "Then I'll run to Asher's for a shower. After that, I'll be back here. What about you?"

"I'll be around here and there," Dillon said. "Olivia has a good handle on running the truck, but I need to head back there for a little while to help her out."

"Sounds good," Billie said. "Let me know how much I owe the plumbers and I'll cut a check."

She had a vague idea of what she wanted to do next but was mostly still troubled about news of the arrest. Something didn't add up to her, but she wasn't sure why. What did she know about any of the people involved, anyway? As far as she knew, Tiffany was a jealous person who killed her business partner in a fit of rage.

Her brief interaction with the woman just before and after the discovery of Kelly's body told her a different story, she supposed. Based on her memory, Tiffany showed no signs of someone upset enough to have killed someone. On the contrary, she appeared to be rather concerned about finding her friend. She'd even complimented her ability to run their mutual business. Those weren't the words of a cold blooded killer.

Of course, the police department had its own

reasons for the arrest. Billie wanted to call Sully and press her for more information. She wanted to hear from the detective herself about the proverbial smoking gun.

She opened her laptop and typed in Kelly Peck's name followed by "Yoga Studios." She was quickly directed to a mystical website with ethereal mist graphics floating over the screen while flute music played. She clicked on several tabs and found bios for both Tiffany and Kelly. The pair had been together for more than ten years. She found pictures of the women smiling with their families, then photos of the women and their families together in one large, smiling group. The photos were less than a year old, according to the date included in the captions.

Nothing about the photos indicated a feud. Instead, each woman's bio spoke of the close friendship that had preceded their business relationship. Of course, it was possible that two best friends might run into hard times. Billie shook her head at the thought of Tiffany murdering her partner.

She clicked another tab marked "events." A calendar popped up with their current schedule. Billie felt a tinge of sadness when she saw her own venue named for the coming weekend. Kelly had no idea going into the weekend that she would never make it back home.

Billie forced herself to focus. She scrolled back several months. Events were common for the pair, it seemed. They had taken their yoga studio on the road to the east coast, then to the west, and two months ago they had spent a week on the island of Maui. "What a tough life," Billie said. She looked out her office window and chuckled at herself. It was easy to say sitting on a tropical island in the Gulf of Mexico herself.

She scanned the various events for anything that stood out to her. Up until then, she had barely paid attention to the name of the event that weekend, aside from the fact that it was called "The Holistic Fair" on the marketing materials for the general public. The name on the contract was a bit longer: "Healing Pathways Presents The Holistic Fair on the Island" was the longer name of the event. Billie noticed another event six months ago under the same name, "Healing Pathways." She clicked on the calendar.

She was directed to another website entirely. The Healing Pathways website event page filled her screen with the message "this event has already passed." The event had taken place in Sacramento, California.

Billie perused the event calendar, which was still up on the website. She found a three-day long itinerary of public yoga classes and demonstrations. Kelly Peck Yoga Studios was listed among the main presenters. While it wasn't clear how old the photos actually were, some of the pictures on the event page included the smiling faces of women she knew, including Tiffany and Kelly herself.

Another face caught her attention. She spotted Whitley Carson in the background.

A list of names was included on the event page. Billie clicked through the list of bios for each of the main vendors. She read the same bios for Tiffany and Kelly that appeared on their company website. Whitley's contained information about her status as a master herbalist and a traditionally trained registered nurse. Billie followed a link to her website, dubbed simply "Whitley Carson, Herbalist."

She focused on Whitley, the woman who complained about Kelly using the water line meant for her own vendor space just before Kelly wound up dead. There was something about that morning that didn't add up for her. When she spotted Whitley, she had been carrying a large case of bottled water, and when the tent flaps opened to her view, Billie noticed three large glass water coolers filled with ice and fruit floating on top. Each of the coolers must have held five gallons of water alone. Each was fitted with a spigot for easy access.

Why on earth did she need a water hose and bottled water if she already had all the other things? Billie couldn't be sure, but decided the only way to find out was to ask her in person.

## CHAPTER 11

"We're not open until morning," Whitley called out when Billie approached her tent.

"I know that," Billie said, moving the tent flap back a few inches. "I was just stopping by to check on you. I wasn't sure if you had heard or not, but access to the commissary kitchen is going to be off limits for the next few hours or so."

"I wasn't aware of the kitchen being open in the first place," Whitely said, eying her doubtfully.

"Well, it technically isn't, but we are a pretty tight knit group around here, and if anyone needed access to hot water or whatever, we're more than likely to make that accommodation for them," she said. It was an outright fib, but Whitley wouldn't have known that.

"Well, thank you anyway, I suppose," she said.

Billie wandered around the interior of the tent. She was amazed at the permanent-looking structures Whitely had erected for the weekend. Wooden counters had been set up around the wall of the tent. Every few feet or so there was a different display that included a small weight scale, glass tea decanters, and paper sample cups. Shelves of glass canisters filled with loose herbs and teas lined the counters. A large wooden island filled the center of the room. The water coolers were on one side and a large sitting area filled the other. Billie counted five bar stools that butted up to the island counter in the center of the room.

"Pardon my curiosity, but what exactly did you need the water hose for?" Billie asked.

Whitley ran her thin hand over her face and pushed loose hair out of her eyes. "I'm afraid I don't know what you're talking about."

"When I saw you earlier, you were in a tizzy over the fact that Kelly had moved the water hose from your tent," Billie said. "You were quite upset with her, as I recall."

"I think you are mistaken," Whitley said. "And if you will excuse me, I have more to do before the fair begins."

Billie walked around the island and stopped. "Are you aware that Tiffany was arrested for Kelly's murder?"

Whitley's face paled. "They arrested Tiffany. When did that happen?" she asked. Her hand immediately went to her chest.

"A little while ago," Billie said. "You didn't know?"

"Not at all," Whitley said, half whispering. "Does anyone else know?"

"I imagine the organizers know, but I'm sure they have asked the police to keep things as quiet as possible."

Whitley stopped. She gazed toward the tent flap, lost in thought. "I need to get things ready for tomorrow," she said again.

"Ms. Carson," Billie said. "Why were you so sure it was Kelly who had displaced the water hose? I know you've probably been to several mutual events like this one. Was there bad blood between you two?"

Her words snapped Whitley out of her daze. "Of course not," she snapped. "What are you getting at? It almost sounds like there is a veiled accusation in there somewhere."

Billie smiled and shook her head. "Not necessarily. It's more like a question. I have to admit, Tiffany and Kelly seemed like the best of friends. How much sense does it make that one would snap and kill the other one?"

Whitley shook her head. "It doesn't make a bit of sense, but I wouldn't have killed her, either. Especially not over a water hose or a tent placement issue. Kelly was my friend, too. She came to me when she was first diagnosed, you know. She wanted to know what natural remedies she could use for her kidneys."

"First diagnosed? What was wrong with her?"

Whitley softened. "Kelly suffered from kidney issues. I assume that's why she died in that hot yoga tent. Too much heat can be deadly for someone in her situation."

"Especially when they are unable to get away from it," Billie said.

"What do you mean by that?" Whitley asked. Her eyebrows were raised in alarm.

"The outfit she wore, the long, flowing layers? When I found her, her feet had been all tangled up in some of the layers," Billie said.

"Kelly always took a little nap for strength after doing anything strenuous," Whitley said. "That wasn't the first time she had chosen the hot tent for her naps."

"But why would her feet be tangled up in her

clothing? It's almost as if someone did that to her on purpose," Billie said, also wondering why she'd choose the hot tent if she struggled being around too much heat. "Clearly, the police think that person was her business partner."

Whitley shook her head. "Tiffany was busy setting up their main tent. That's why when I saw the water hose going to the hot yoga tent, I assumed it was Kelly's doing instead of Tiffany's. Even though Kelly doesn't do the yoga portion of their business, she's the one who designed the sauna to work for the tent.

I thought for sure that she'd woken up from her rest and started getting things ready."

"I still don't buy that Tiffany killed her partner, but who else could have had any reason for it?"

"You mean aside from me?" Whitley asked ruefully. "You might want to check with the event organizers to see if you can get an answer to that question. None of them were great fans of Kelly's. They loved Tiffany, but something about Kelly put them off."

"What do you mean?" Billie asked.

"I mean Kelly wasn't everyone's cup of tea," Whitley said. "She was a larger woman with eccentric tastes. There is an image Healing Pathways prefers for its more visible partners. I fit that image. Tiffany fits that image."

"But Kelly did not," Billie said. "Still, would that really be the motive to kill her?"

"All I can tell you is that there was a scene a few months ago in California," Whitley said. "It had something to do with Kelly's illness and appearance. I don't think the organizers wanted Kelly out in front any longer with their yoga presentations for the public. They preferred Tiffany. She is more in tune with their image."

## CHAPTER 12

"How are things going?" Asher asked Billie when she answered her phone on the way back to the commissary kitchen.

"If you're asking whether or not the fair is going to open in the morning, the answer is yes," Billie said.

"That's good, but I'm really asking how you're doing."

"I'm okay."

"Somehow, I don't buy that," he said.

"Sully arrested the partner of the victim for her murder," Billie said.

"Let me guess. You're not buying it?" Asher said.

"Not one bit," Billie said. "I just spoke with the woman who Kelly, the victim, had a disagreement with. In fact, this same woman was looking for her because she was upset with her just before I found her body."

"Billie, promise me you're being careful," Asher said.

"I promise," Billie said. "I'm just asking questions."

"Okay, but you need to watch your back," Asher said. "I called Dillon a little while ago. He told me about the water."

"Yeah, he's been amazing," Billie said. She opened the heavy metal door to the building and let it close behind her.

"Hey, Billie, I was just thinking," Asher said. "You said earlier that there was an issue about where the water hose was right before the woman was found dead. Where did they find the hose?"

"Next to the hot yoga tent where the body was found," Billie said. "Why do you ask?"

"What was the victim even using the hose for?" he asked her.

"I suppose it was the water source for the sauna," Billie said.

"Okay but a true sauna doesn't require a lot of water. I don't know what kind of tent this is or anything, but I doubt there would be a need for the entire hose," Asher said. "Maybe a bucket of water with a ladle in it."

"There was definitely too much water in that sauna. Water was pooled all over the place."

"Then I would assume your killer deliberately overheated the place," Asher said. "For what reason, I have no idea."

"Yeah, and I just found out that the victim had kidney trouble," she said. "That can cause all sorts of issues."

"Didn't you tell me that her feet were all wrapped up, too?"

"Yes, and it turns out she had a habit of taking a nap in the hot tent before events," she said.

"So, if someone else knew that, they'd also know overheating the place while she was inside of it would be bad for her."

Billie wondered who else knew about her napping spot.

"The woman I talked to this morning told me I should look into the organizers for more answers. It sounds like there was a history there."

"I spoke with them quite a bit over the past few months," Asher said. "Of course, it was only over the phone, but there was one of them who seemed to be fairly preoccupied with making sure everything was just right. The whole group seemed pretty preoccupied with their image as well."

"I met them. Tara and Myrtle both seemed fairly worried about it," Billie said.

"Really? I thought it was the man, Hector, who seemed the most preoccupied with it. He really wanted to make sure the grounds would add to the appearance of good health and wellness," Asher said. "I mean, I get it. He's a practitioner himself."

"Hector is a practitioner? Of what?"

"Yeah, he's a reflexologist," Asher said.

Billie rushed to her office with the phone in her ear. She pulled her laptop lid open and googled Hector Jamison's name. She immediately found a website for his reflexology practice. "I found his website," she told Asher. "He has great reviews."

"I would imagine so," Asher said. "He was very clear about how highly respected his practice is. The holistic fair was his idea in the first place, I think."

"I wonder how he wound up paired with the other two," Billie mused.

"Hey, Billie, I'm sorry but I need to run," Asher said. "I'll be home in three days. See you then."

Billie said her goodbyes and continued to study the website. After a few minutes, she returned to the search result page and scrolled through a few pages of results. She was in search of something, but she was still not sure what.

A few minutes later, she found what she had been looking for. Billie quickly took a screenshot of an online exchange between Hector and Kelly on a wellness message board, then printed off the page. She snatched the page from her printer and immediately dialed Detective Sullivan.

"Sully, I need you to head back over to the festival grounds as soon as you get this," Billie said when the voicemail picked up. "I think you arrested the wrong person. I'll be near their tents." She pushed her phone back into her back pocket and headed outside.

She went straight for the hot yoga tent where she had found Kelly's body. Yellow police tape still surrounded the structure, but Billie was more interested in the outside of the tent. She recalled from her brief visit to the tent that the sauna heater was positioned at the back of the tent. Billie pulled out her phone again and turned on her flashlight. She slipped beside the tent and the space next to it and walked sideways until she made it to the back. She turned the corner and stepped carefully between the yoga tent and the tent behind it.

Billie held her phone in one hand and felt carefully along the back of the tent with the second. She paused when she felt a slit in the canvas, just large enough to slip a water hose through. She turned on her camera app and carefully snapped a few photos of the slit.

"Billie?" Sully's voice called to her in the distance.

"I'm here," Billie said. "Be out in a second." She backed herself out of the space between the tents and headed out to the walkway.

"What are you doing back there?" Sully asked.

"I had a hunch," she said. She showed Sully the pictures. "I think someone cut a slit in the back of the tent and shoved the water hose through it and into the sauna heater."

"Interesting," Sully said. She took the phone from Billie and studied the photos. "But that doesn't exactly exonerate Tiffany."

"No, but it does beg the question, why would she cut a hole in her own tent?"

Sully nodded. "I'm afraid that isn't enough to prove anything," she said.

"Well, maybe this is." Billie pulled the printout from the website out of her pocket and handed it to the detective. "I found these six or seven pages in a google search for Hector Jamison."

"What is this?"

"It's from the wellness section of a popular message board," Billie said. "I believe this is an argument between Kelly and Hector." She pointed out each person's profile and icon.

"'I think it would be best for you to have your partner conduct the public yoga classes,'" Sully read aloud. She looked up at Billie. "This is Jamison speaking?"

Billie nodded. "Right, and he is addressing Kelly directly," she said. "'That is unfair, discriminatory, and not part of our agreement.'"

"She used the word 'discriminatory,'" Sully said. "Interesting."

"Read a little further." Billie pointed to another section of conversation down the page. "It's not my fault I have a medical condition now."

"But it is your fault if your appearance casts a shadow over our event," Sully read. "He wanted her to hide in the shadows because she was sick?"

"He knew she had kidney problems, Sully," Billie said. "I know it is a stretch, but he is a reflexologist. I think he offered to work on her feet for her. She fell asleep and he tied her flowy skirts around her feet so she couldn't get up, then upped the heat in the tent hoping she was going to feel bad enough that she would think twice about leading the yoga class tomorrow."

Sully turned around with her hands on her hips and nodded her head slowly. "Okay, well, I think you might have just solved a mystery you didn't even know about."

"What are you talking about?" Billie asked.

"The coroner found something on the victim's feet none of us could explain, and I think you accidentally just did," Sully said.

"What did he find?"

"Castor oil. It was up and down her feet all the way to her ankles."

"How does this solve a mystery?" Billie asked.

"Castor oil is often used by reflexologists during their treatment practice," Sully said. "I think we need to have a look at Hector Jamison's vendor site."

## CHAPTER 13

"I don't get it," Isa said early the next morning. She walked around the test kitchen with a knife in her hand.

"What don't you get?" Billie asked.

"I don't understand how Detective Sullivan figured out Hector was the killer just from the oil on the victim's feet," Isa said.

"She explained it earlier," Rhonda said from the other side of the counter. The older woman watched the young chef slice up her peppers and onions with keen interest. "It wasn't the fact that Kelly had oil on her feet that led to his arrest. It was the fact that they found oily fingerprints on the water hose."

"I think he knew the prints would match his," Dillon said.

"And he wanted to get out ahead of it and tell his side of the story," Billie said.

"What's his side of the story? He killed her. He doesn't deserve to have a side," Isa said.

"He insists that it was an accident," Billie said. "He plans to argue that he only meant to make her sick by heating up the tent. He didn't know she would decline so quickly."

"What was the actual cause of death?" Polly asked.

"Organ failure," Billie said. She pulled a chair up to the outside counter next to the neighboring kitchen.

"I'm sorry, but I can't keep talking about this while I'm cooking," Isa said.

"Right." Billie nodded. "What are you making today, Toren?"

"I had a request from someone in the audience for a demonstration of my famous burgers," Toren said.

The first day of sales for his vegan truck had beaten all expectations. He winked at Rhonda and turned back to the cutting board. He chopped four large portobello mushrooms into fine pieces. "Some chefs like to sauté the mushrooms for moisture, but I keep them raw."

"Why is that?" Polly asked. She pulled a chair over next to Billie and sat down.

"Well, because I like my burgers meaty and not too smooth. Chopping them up raw resembles the meat in burgers," Toren said. As soon as he finished chopping the mushrooms, he started on the broccoli and onions. "I like to smash the black beans with a fork for the same reason."

"Texture," Polly said.

"Exactly." Toren smiled at her. Billie looked between the two and wondered if there might be a match in the making.

"Very interesting," Rhonda said from where she was seated.

"Next I mix everything together and add gluten free bread crumbs and an egg substitute," Toren explained.

"What seasonings are you using?" Polly asked.

"Well, I mix salt and pepper in with some smoky paprika and a bit of liquid smoke," Toren explained. He picked up a handful of the mixture and began forming a patty. "I like to use a splash of vegan Worcestershire sauce and vegan parmesan as well."

"I smell garlic," Billie said.

"You didn't see him chopping up the garlic cloves?" Polly asked her.

"Apparently she wasn't watching as close as you were," Rhonda teased. Polly immediately turned red.

Billie watched with amusement while Toren formed more patties and set them in the hot, cast iron skillet. The entire space filled with the aromas of a sizzling grill at an outdoor cookout. Toren skillfully flipped the burgers after they browned. He tossed a burger in the air and caught it on a plate on top of an open bun, then he slid the plate in front of Rhonda.

"Oh, how fancy," Rhonda said, clapping her hands together.

"Now tell me, Miss Rhonda," Toren said. "How does this compare to a hamburger grilled outdoors?"

She scooped the burger up off of the plate and took a huge bite. "Mmmmm," she said and closed her eyes.

"I think that says it all," Billie said. She looked up and smiled at a familiar redhead walking down the hall toward the kitchen space. "Good morning, Sully."

"Morning, all." Sully smiled. "What are we doing here?"

"Making grilled vegan burgers." Toren slid the next plate over to her.

Sully smiled and studied the plate. "I am a carnivore, through and through," she said. "Give me a good reason to try this."

"It's delicious," Polly said.

"It really is terrific," Rhonda said.

"Not to mention, it's much better for your heart," Toren said.

Sully rolled her eyes and picked up the burger. She took a big bite and set the burger back down on the plate. "Hmmmm," she said.

"Well? What do you think?" Billie asked.

"Yeah, don't keep us in suspense," Rhonda said.

"Well," Sully said. "It's not exactly like a grilled burger, but it is amazing. I don't think I will replace burgers with this, but I would like to add this to my diet."

Polly, Isa, Rhonda, and everyone else began clapping. Toren stepped away from the stove and took a sweeping bow. Sully picked up the burger and took another large bite and smiled. She turned to Billie.

"I just thought I would let you know, Tiffany was released from county jail early this morning," Sully told her. "She went straight back to her home in Seattle."

Billie nodded her head. "I imagine she did," she said.

"And I can't imagine that she wanted to hang around the place much longer," Rhonda added.

Sully shook her head. "I think she left her tents set

up and told the remaining organizers to shove it when they complained about it."

"That sounds like some very specific information," Isa said.

"Let's just say that I heard it through the grapevine," Sully said. "I also heard that Tara and Myrtle are doing their level best to separate themselves from Hector. I have seen them making the rounds already this morning."

"Making the rounds?" Billie asked.

"Tara and Myrtle checking in on each of their vendors, one at a time, just to make sure everyone is alright," Sully said. "I think there will be quite a bit of image softening over the next few days."

"Makes me wonder how they're going to act when they see your face," Rhonda mused.

"What do you mean?" Billie asked.

"You're the one who put things together and figured out who the real murderer was, right?" Rhonda asked. She cast a sideways look at Sully. "Unless that's a secret you're keeping under wraps right now."

"We're not keeping it under wraps, per se," Sully said. "But I think it might be a good idea to keep things quiet for the time being. It will all come out in time. Billie doesn't need any more trouble right now."

She smiled. "That's for sure," she said. "I have enough on my plate pretending like I know what I'm doing with Asher gone anyway. And I better not find out that a single one of you told him I said that."

\*\*\*

If you enjoyed One Fell Soup and are looking for more food truck adventures, check out Wurst Day Ever, today!

# AUTHOR'S NOTE

I'd love to hear your thoughts on my books, the storylines, and anything else that you'd like to comment on—reader feedback is very important to me. My contact information, along with some other helpful links, is listed on the next page. If you'd like to be on my list of "folks to contact" with updates, release and sales notifications, etc.… just shoot me an email and let me know. Thanks for reading!

Also…

… if you're looking for more great reads, Summer Prescott Books publishes several popular series by outstanding Cozy Mystery authors.

# CONTACT GRETCHEN ALLEN

Visit my website for more information about new releases, upcoming projects, and be sure to check out my special Members Only section for extra freebies and fun!

Website: www.gretchenallen.com

Email: contact@gretchenallen.com

Visit the Summer Prescott Books website to find even more great reads!

Made in the USA
Coppell, TX
06 May 2023